ANYWHERE BUT HERE

Also by Jordon Greene

Novels
They'll Call It Treason
To Watch You Bleed

JORDON GREENE

ANY WHERE BUT HERE

FRANKLIN/KERR

CONCORD, NORTH CAROLINA

ANYWHERE BUT HERE. Copyright © 2017 by Jordon Greene. All rights reserved. No part of this book may be reproduced, stored in a retrieval system, or transmitted in any way by any means, electronic, mechanical, photocopy, recording or otherwise without prior written permission except in the case of brief quotations embodied in critical articles and reviews or as provided by US copyright law.

Published by Franklin/Kerr Press, LLC
349-L Copperfield Boulevard #502 | Concord, North Carolina 28025
1.704.659.3915 | info@franklinkerr.com
www.FranklinKerr.com

Edited by Chelly Peeler
Cover & Interior design by Jordon Greene

Printed in the United States of America

FIRST EDITION

ISBN-10: 0-9983913-2-8
ISBN-13: 978-0-9983913-2-8

Fiction: Horror
Fiction: Psychological Thriller
Fiction: Thriller

To Tammy Cook-Sanabria
or as I knew you, Ms. Hicks, my sixth grade teacher.
It was in your class that I first started to write stories and
you went out of your way to foster my love for the
written word. Thank you for your continued
support through all these years.

ACKNOWLEDGMENTS

If it hadn't been for a conversation with my little brother about night terrors this story probably wouldn't be here today. So, to start, I'd like to thank my little brother, Jared Greene, for prompting the idea behind this story and telling me how much the idea horrified him. That's about all I needed to hear to get started.

Thanks, as always, to my mother, Kim Greene, who was an integral part again in developing the main character. She was also very helpful with some of the plot elements, though I did try to keep my mouth shut this time so she could read it without knowing the story first. I failed on that part a little bit.

Mike Wagner came back for yet another round of beta reading and was joined by Heather Lovins, David Kummer and Michael Blackbourn. Thank you all for your help! I'd like to say a special thanks to Michael Blackbourn, who really combed through the story and helped me push it up to the next level.

You might not think putting together a synopsis is hard after writing a book, but it is. I'm glad to have had help with forming mine from John Gjertsen and Eileen Beucler Franklin.

A big thanks goes to my proofreader, Graham, over in the UK. Of course, I cannot forget to thank my absolutely amazing editor, Chelly Hoyle Peeler. You are a godsend.

1

My eyes ratchet open to an empty ceiling cast in grim shadows. A shiver overtakes my leg and clambers up my spine. Hasty bursts of crystallized mist form above my lips and vanish with each labored breath.

I swear the ceiling is moving, alive. Void of any real form, it shifts and morphs. The bland water-stained tiles almost seem to phase in and out of existence, between the dirty white and an all-consuming blackness.

No. The ceiling isn't moving. I focus more intently, shivering inside. I'm so exposed, open to whatever blackness it is that lurks above. Finally, it seems to clear up in my mind. It's not the ceiling that moves and writhes. It's a dark, almost tangible-looking fog. It moves, squirms, pushes and pulls against itself along some contradictory current. Even though I refuse to touch it, I know I can feel it. Pulsing, unnatural.

I reach to do what just moments ago was the unthinkable, to touch the writhing fog, but my arm doesn't move. I wrinkle my brow in confusion and try again. Nothing. My mind begins to race as I realize I can't control my arms, my legs, my body, only my eyes thrash in their sockets. I strain to move, inside I'm rocking like a raging sea. I need to move, if only to wiggle a finger, a toe, to turn my head, anything. The more I try, the more fear and aggravation builds in my chest. What's happening?

Click. Click.

My eyes dart toward the right corner of the room, drawn to the noise, but I can only see the upper quarter where the two walls meet.

The fog is moving down the wall, enveloping the blossom-patterned wallpaper at a slow and deliberate pace. I squint as the shadow-cast crimson yellow and blue blossoms slowly wilt under the encroaching fog. I swear they wither to dead brown petals in front of my eyes under the fog's grasp, like the very life is being sucked from their roots. It's impossible, but I'm sure of it all the same.

Click. Click.

There it is again, this time to my right, and closer. My eyes dart to the opposite side of the bed where the room's only light source casts a faint glow against the closest wall and an even fainter glow against the growing darkness above. An IV pump, its clear tubes drape over its side, disappearing somewhere below. Where am I?

I try to calm my breathing as the fog grows denser and a sense of claustrophobia sets in. I have to calm down. I have to figure out what's going on. My eyes flick back and forth in their sockets, trying to see within the constraints imposed by my immobile body.

A subtle movement breaches the edge of my vision, drawing my attention. My eyes snap to the corner. Without thinking I drag a gulp of air into my lungs and in a slow stutter, release it again as my eyes lock on to *the figure.*

I can't see much, but I don't need to. It's black, like the fog, but with a grotesque, more defined form. I can only see the top half of its head. Those empty eyes. Black voids where two intricate eyes should be. Even still I feel its gaze boring into my mind. I feel it in bones, in my stomach.

I can't break its stare, freezing in place the only part of my body I have any control over. I want to run. Instead, I watch like a deer in headlights, helpless, examining the pulsing black sinew of its head as it stands stoically in the corner, boring its sockets at me.

An eternity passes, my only sensation is the beat of my heart punching the inside of my chest. The form stands motionless. It stares.

I count my heartbeats.

One. Two. Three. Fo…

It moves.

I pour all my will into lifting my head, screaming inside to jump off the bed as the figure steps forward a singular long footstep, but nothing happens. I can feel my body. I can feel my head and arms, my legs hanging limply, like they *should* have moved, but nothing happens as the figure advances again.

I beg for anything to bellow out from between my lips, to scream as loud as I can manage, to hold out my hands as if I could somehow hold back the thing that approaches. It's useless. Not a sound escapes my mouth and not a muscle twitches under my skin. I'm not even sure whether my lips are parted. It moves a step closer, like some slow-motion movie.

Then suddenly it disappears. My chest burns as it rises and falls with each breath while I lie helpless on this godforsaken bed.

Where'd it go?

I search the room, that which I can see at least. I take in the roiling fog as it continues to move further down the wall, seeming to digest the very structure around me. It's past my vision now. I can imagine it swirling against the floor, blanketing everything it touches.

Click. Click.

My eyes shoot to the left where the noise originated. *It's closer.* A deep chill envelopes my arms and body, a geyser of warm breath hitting cold air bursts from my mouth. I want to close my eyes, but I'm horrified to let my guard down. Instead I push my pupils to their limits, trying to capture as much of the room as I can, needing some sign of where the figure is, or if it's anywhere at all.

I force myself to count the beats of my heart, focusing on its rhythm. *One. Two.* I keep counting. The room is silent. *Fourteen. Fifteen.* The fog continues to slither over the walls, thrumming quietly, and I lose count. I shake my head, trying to refocus. There's no noise, no movement, no figure. I know it's in here somewhere though. I try to move with every ounce of energy I can muster, but it gets me nowhere. My breathing is rapid, quick bursts between horrified swallows punctuate each dart of my eyes.

Without warning the room goes deathly silent. Even the constant hum of the machines next to my bed ceases, leaving me enveloped in nothing but a pitch-black room covered in an unnatural fog…and something else. The sound of my shaking breath is unbearable as I search the room, straining to hear any slight hint of movement.

Then I feel a hot breath against my ear.

I scream inside! I beg with everything I have to escape, to get away from this place. I feel my finger move and a sliver of noise escapes my lips. A glimmer of hope in the darkness. It isn't much, but it's everything to me. Abruptly the fog vanishes, replaced by the dingy ceiling tiles and colorful wallpaper.

Finally, all the fear inside my body breaches my lips and I scream in horror as movement reaches my hand and body. I shoot up in bed, heaving, begging for air.

I clamp my eyes shut and let my breathing relax as a noise touches my ear. I turn my head toward the opening door, every muscle in my body tensing. I start to shrink back when a woman clothed in teal nursing garb slips through the door at a near jog. She flicks on the lights and lets the door slap shut behind her. Her face is worried. Thin, unpainted lips frown down at me as her bright blue eyes reach my own.

"Are you okay, Mr. Evans?" she asks. Her concerned but somehow calm voice is disarming.

For a moment, I don't answer. I'm still shaken by how real my dream felt. I rock my head from side-to-side, trying to cement myself back into reality, away from the darkness and the demons of the night world.

"Uh. Yeah." The words are weak, barely a whisper between my lips, further extenuating the shrill quality of my fading Welsh accent. Frankly, I don't care at the moment. My body is still shaking, as is my voice. I wrap my arms around my flat chest, too frazzled to think about the sheets lying in my lap. I rock my head back and forth for a moment, then force my eyes up to the ceiling, attempting to validate that I'm no longer dreaming, checking for the pulsing black fog. It's not there. I'm awake, actually awake. I exhale. It was all a dream, but it was a damned real dream.

"I take it you had an episode?"

I can tell she's trying to tread lightly by the way her right eye squints and the edge of her lip under the same eye rises. I nod and glance at her name tag. Vickie. I want to speak but I'm winded and weak as the adrenaline dissipates from my veins.

"Well, I think we got it on record this time," Vickie tells me, shrinking away from my side. She moves around the foot of the bed to check the machines hooked up to my body on my opposite side. I'd forgotten about the pads stuck to my forehead, arms, and bared chest. Stupidly I feel self-conscience and pull up the bed sheets to cover myself. Vickie grins, probably wondering why a boy my age would even care, but acts as though she hadn't noticed. I chide myself. It's not like there was anything to notice. I wouldn't exactly call my body impressive.

"So, we'll keep monitoring you through to the morning so we can get a full night on record," Vickie explains. She looks down at her wrist where a simple brown watch rests and then back up to me with a faint smile. "You've got a few more hours, it's only three in the morning. I'm glad we got your night terror on record, but hopefully you'll be able to get some sleep now."

"Yeah." It felt pathetic to just say *yeah*, but it's all that came to mind. The figure in my dream still plagues my thoughts. I've never seen more than its eyes, just like always, but the breath against my ear… I shiver. I've never felt that before, not until tonight.

"Thanks." I force the words from my lips. "Um…yeah, some regular sleep would be nice."

The nurse smiles and walks away, but stops before exiting the room. She turns back around and grins lightly.

"Get some sleep, Mr. Evans. I'll wake you around seven."

2

"Mr. Evans."

A quiet voice vibrates in my ear just before my eyelids separate. They open like a shuttered window and the nurse from last night comes into view. I can't remember her name.

"Good morning, Taren." She uses my first name, letting her volume increase as if she had to be quiet to wake me.

"Morning," I croak and rise to my elbows.

Before I can utter another word, she rounds the bed and is already about removing the electrodes stuck to my body. I twitch as one of the sticky pads pulls at a few hairs on my arm. I can't complain much though, it's not like there is much there to pull. My parents had told me when I was younger that I'd grow some hair on my arms and chest when I grew older. Well, I'm nineteen now and the best I have going for me is a few colorless strands on my arms. Not exactly impressive.

"So, did you sleep well last night after that episode?" the nurse asks.

I glance at her, trying to catch a glimpse of her name tag without the obvious giveaway that I don't remember her name. I fail, but the point is I found her name. She smiles but makes nothing else of it.

"Yes, Vickie, I did actually." I say her name much too loud. What am I doing? I have a girlfriend. A gorgeous girlfriend. Why is this young nurse making me nervous? I sigh and chalk it up to hormones and move on, "It was all smooth sailing once I got back to sleep."

"Very good." She nods. "If you don't mind me asking, what do you see when you have your night terrors?"

I force a grin and look up at her. Everyone wonders what it's like when you wake in the middle of the night paralyzed and hallucinating beyond your control. I'm finally getting used to the question.

"I'm not sure really. I just know it's… uh…" I search for the right word. Finally, I find it and give her a whimsical smile to make myself not sound so crazy as I continue to explain, "Evil. Yeah, I guess evil is the word for it. It's some dark figure, but I've never seen more than a glimpse of it."

I happily leave out the rest. *It* moving closer. *Its* hideous empty face. The encroaching ravenous fog all around me. *Its* hot breath against my ear. It's all so silly now that I'm awake, and even worse revealing it to someone else, but it sure as hell felt fucking real while I lay paralyzed in bed.

"I'm not sure I could stand that." Vickie makes a show of shivering and blinks as she removes the last of the electrodes, tucking them into the neighboring machine. "I do hope Dr. Gillespie can help. I'm sure it's all a matter of finding the right treatment, Taren."

I nod. I'd heard that same line plenty of times over the past two years, since so many of my nights morphed into real life nightmares and I learned about my sleep disorder, sleep paralysis. It *literally* haunts me. At first the night terrors were short and simple, for the most part. I swear they've only further devolved into madness and horror though, even with all the treatments, the prescription meds, time with the shrink.

"I know." I put on a fake grin. "I guess we'll see soon. And I'm sure you could deal with it. It's not like you'd have much of a choice though, really."

She doesn't say anything to that and I immediately regret my words. I didn't realize how pathetic and self-loathing it sounded until it exited my lips. I try to make up for it.

"So, I guess I'm good to go then?" I end on a happier note.

"Oh, yes. I just have to get your paperwork ready, I believe Dr. Gillespie wants to see you back here next Monday," she says then heads for the door. "I'll be right back."

I nod as she leaves and then fall back to the stiff hospital mattress. How the hell did I sleep on this thing? I'm inclined to blame the new bit of my night terror on its rigid support, but that'd be a reach. With that thought, I throw back the blankets that covered my mostly naked body, except for the gray boxer briefs, and climb out of the bed.

The laminate floor bites at my toes, cold against the bare pads of my feet as I make my way to the small bathroom and shut the door behind me. My belongings are still sitting in the corner as I left them. I pick up the wad of clothes and get dressed, donning a Carolina t-shirt with our ram mascot emblazoned proudly on the chest and a pair of faded blue jeans. I'm not the biggest sports fanatic, I mean I did play high school basketball for a whole eight minutes my freshman year, but how can you not support your school team, especially when it's the Tarheels?

I peer into the mirror. My eyes meet their reflection and I shiver. The nightmare was never really gone, not when it was so real. I force the dark figure from my mind, at least for the moment. My eyes glide over my taut pale skin. I reach to my forehead to wipe away the black residue left behind by the electrodes.

All the gunk scrubbed from my head and chest, I take a quick look in the mirror and swipe a hand through my messy black hair. It doesn't help much, it never does really, but I like the messy look. I try to ignore the graying circles around my eyes but it's hard when they contrast so much with my crystal blues and seem to make my face appear thinner than it already is. I hear the other door creak open so I slip on my shoes and slide back out into the main room. Vickie is standing patiently with my papers. I grin.

"You're all set to go." She hands me the papers and moments later I'm exiting the clinic doors and getting situated in my golden Honda Accord.

I press the ignition button and the car hums to life. I'd like to say roars or rumbles to life, but I don't think that's in this car's vocabulary. I check the digital dash clock. *7:36am. Good, just enough time to make it to the diner.*

Morgan, my girlfriend, wanted to have breakfast before her nine-thirty class, something about American history. Being that today is one of the few times I'm already up this early, she was certain to demand breakfast. Truth be told, I had hoped for a nap, but how could I say no to those gorgeous brown eyes? Hell, I'll probably doze off during my English lecture this afternoon anyway. It was one of the few, and only, perks of narcolepsy.

Ten minutes later, I park up close to Mama Dip's Kitchen, a local diner off West Rosemary Street, just under two miles from Morgan's dorm room on campus and the clinic. I'm early and Mama Dip's doesn't open until eight so I lean my seat back and roll my windows down. I can smell the greasy hash browns and bacon and imagine my plate.

Even this early in the morning the summer air is warm, well, tepid maybe. By midday, the combined heat and humidity is sure to elicit a little sweat out of me.

I recline back and let one of my favorite metalcore bands distract me with glorious riffs and screams while I wait for Morgan to arrive and Mama Dip's to open. I'm about to close my eyes before I hear another car pull up. Brakes screech ever so lightly and I lean up to see who it is. I smile. Morgan grins back at me and waves as she gets out of her car.

"Morning." I greet her as I do the same. I lock my car doors with a tiny chirp. She has her hair down. I love how those long bronze locks wave over her shoulders and frame her pink smile.

"Good morning," she replies.

I gather her up in my arms and pull her to me, leaning back against my car for support. Her body presses against mine, I kiss her, "A very good morning." I grin and she chuckles. It's a cute laugh, nothing obnoxious, but cute.

"Oh, calm down, Taren," Morgan chides me, biting her lip.

"You want me to calm down and you go and bite your lip?" I ask, eyes wide, grinning from cheek-to-cheek. "That's pretty impossible."

I lean back in and kiss her again, tasting her pink lips. I let go and she props her forehead against mine and just grins.

"So, how'd the sleep study go?" she asks, unable to wipe that beautiful grin from her lips.

"Well…uh…" I start, stuttering like some damned fool.

"Did you have a night terror?" she interrupts. I can see it her eyes, she knows I did.

I nod, confirming what she already knew and give her a sheepish sideways grin. "Yeah."

"Well, that's good, right?" she asks, trying to make something good of the impossibly dreadful. "I mean it sucks but that's the whole point of the study, isn't it?"

"Yeah, it is. It's just…" I scour my mind for the right words. It shouldn't be so hard to explain, but it feels stupid to say I was afraid. I should've just told her at the beginning and not let my mind get me into this rut. I stare at the ground in shame. "It's just that it's not exactly an exciting thing…well, it's pretty damn exciting actually, just not in the way you'd like. You know what I'm getting at. I hate it. It doesn't matter who you are, it's scary, that's all."

I feel the warmth of Morgan's palm on my cheek as she lifts my face to look into her eyes, a brilliant mix of a deep brown surrounded by amber. I'm supposed to be the strong one, but here I am pouting over a dream. I hate myself for this weakness, even if there is little I can do about it.

"Of course it's scary, Taren," she says caringly. "From everything you've told me about it, I can only imagine. Don't be ashamed of that."

I try to lower my head again but Morgan moves in and caresses her cheek against mine and hugs me. "I love you no matter what. Now let's get some breakfast."

3

"Ben Affleck is easily the best Batman," Matthew O'Shea asserts.

Asher and I just stare back at him with brows raised as the opening scene of *The Dark Knight* rolls onto the fifty-inch flat screen.

"Well, at least he didn't say George Clooney," Asher Perry jokes, playfully knocking his shoulder against mine. I take the impact with a laugh, sitting next to him on the old couch closest to the kitchen. Matthew, or Matt as most call him, is more sprawled out than sitting on the couch next to us.

"Yeah, really," I laugh. "It could have been worse I guess."

"Seriously, guys? You don't think Affleck is an awesome Batman?" Matt asks. He's obviously determined, as he always is, about every opinion he holds. His dark green eyes are lit up with surprise.

I pause the movie before it can get too far. No one's going to be watching Batman for at least a few minutes. I look over at Matt with a grin, trying not to laugh.

"Sure, he's a great Batman, but I mean what about Bale? I mean sure, everyone gives him shit for his Batman voice, but it makes sense and he did such a good job."

"Yeah, I agree with Taren," Asher pipes in, his pale skin and long nose shifting in the overhead light as he maneuvers around to face Matt. If Rohan, our other roommate, wasn't away on campus for his Wednesday night class, something about server-side programming, I'm fairly certain he'd be siding with Asher and me. "I'd say the scale is something like Bale, Affleck, Kilmer, Keaton, West and Clooney in dead last."

"Don't forget Will Arnett." Matt added to the list.

"Arnett?" I ask, casting a confused look over my face.

"Yeah, Lego Batman," he answered. "He's awesome!"

"Yeah, I'd put him just behind Affleck." Asher decided with a nod.

"Seriously?" I ask, chuckling.

"Of course, Lego Batman is great!"

We all laugh. Poor Clooney. Even Lego Batman usurped his superhero throne.

"Good point. Not sure I'd put Clooney that far down on the list, but it's hard to compare West's Batman with any of the others." I step in to defend Clooney finally, someone should, he is a great actor. It just wasn't the role for him.

"Good point," Matt agrees.

"Why don't we stop talking about Batman and watch him instead?" Asher suggests, clearly ready to get into movie mode.

Matt nods and I resume the movie. Before the high-rise window could even shatter and the movie officially begin, Matt is out of his seat. I turn and put my hands up, palms out, as if to ask *what?*

"We forgot the chips and drinks." Matt jumps around the couch and makes his way off toward the kitchen. "Go ahead and start it and I'll get it all ready, I like the new movies better anyway."

I roll my eyes and smile, resuming the film yet again. As the movie plays, the sound of a microwave coming to life joins the shotgun blasts and screaming on the screen. Minutes later, Matt saunters in with a huge plateful of nachos in one hand and three tall PBR cans balanced in his other hand.

"What'd you do? Use the whole damn bag?" I ask, staring at the nacho platter. It's piled high with glorious mounds of cheddar cheese drizzled chips peppered with hot sauce.

"Shh." Asher hushes us; his eyes are glued to the television screen.

I grin at Matt, who is doing likewise, and accept the beer before leaning back against the old couch.

An hour passes and the chips plate is empty and we've each downed another PBR. On the television screen the Joker is pissing off the mob. My eyes are already beginning to get heavy.

"Hey, guys." Matt interrupts the movie and holds up his phone. "Have you guys seen this?"

Asher and I both look up with eyebrows raised for the second time tonight.

"What?" I ask, failing to hide my irritation. I hate it when people talk during movies. I won't even go to the movies until the movie has been out for a good two weeks, and even then, it must be early and the room devoid of people and their disrespectful mid-movie chitchat. I take my movies seriously.

"There was a murder nearby." Matt stares at his phone and taps the screen a few times. "There, take a look."

I feel my phone vibrate in my pocket and huff as I retrieve it, pausing the movie with my free hand. I flick the screen open and quickly find the message Matt just sent me, and apparently, Asher too from the looks of it.

"Crazy," Matt keeps on.

I click the link and skim through the story. A grimace forms across my face. A family of four murdered in their sleep in Raleigh. Cut open and left to die. No known motive. At least the article doesn't claim to know one yet, and no suspect. I look at the date. It had happened two days ago, just hours before my night terror in the hospital on Monday.

"Ugh," Asher grunts. "It happens all the time though."

I nod in the dark before Matt responds. "But look how close. I mean that's only like what, twenty, maybe thirty minutes from here, right?"

"Yeah, but it's Raleigh," I reason, dismissing the assertion. "That type of thing isn't all that uncommon. I mean, it's horrible, but it happens in the big cities. We're in Chapel Hill, I think *we're* fine."

"Yeah, I mean, I know." Matt tries to pick up the pieces of his pride. "I just thought it was crazy."

"Well, if anyone comes here, we're safe anyway, right?" Asher says more than asks. "I mean you do have a pistol in your room, against state law and all, but you do, right?"

I hide a grin at Asher's concern as his words morph from the comical to the serious while trying not to sound needy or terrified. I shake my head.

Matt smiles widely and nods. That's not all Matt hides in his room that the University wouldn't exactly be pleased with, or the cops for that matter. Weed isn't exactly legal here, yet. I grin lightly and continue to shake my head.

"How about we get back to the movie?" I suggest. Matt and Asher nod and I start the movie again. An hour and a half later, the credits are rolling and my heavy, sleep deprived lids are winning the fight. Any longer on the couch and I'd be asleep and trying to spoon with Asher. I shiver at the thought. *Hell no.*

I slouch forward and get to my feet, "I'm calling it a night, guys."

"Why so tired?" Asher tries in his best, yet still failing, Joker voice.

I glare at him, half in and half out of sleep, and huff as much amusement as I can muster with a small grin. Matt chuckles and I turn and make my exit from the living room to my small bedroom. I barely miss kneeing the tiny excuse for a desk by the door as I shut the door behind me and pass to my bed without even turning the lights on.

Man am I tired. It's out of my control now as I manage to shove my jeans off before I collapse on the bed and the world starts to fade into beautiful sleep seconds later.

4

I gasp and open my eyes but my lips remain still. A black fog blankets the ceiling, writhing and moving with no defined rhythm.

I close my eyes, wishing the fog away, hoping it's just a figment of my imagination, some memory of a past night terror. I let my eyes part. It's still there, moving along the ceiling. I can feel it deep inside my chest. It's like someone dropped a body builder's barbell on my chest to hold me down. I try to move but I get nowhere.

Despite the wide chasm separating me from its ebony sinews, my chest is heavy under the fog. I strain for breath, begging for the weight to be lifted from my body, before finally the feeling eases. I try to move again but my body doesn't respond. Paralyzed.

I panic. Inside I thrash in horror, begging to move, pleading with my legs, my arms, any part of me to animate. I can still feel my body. A chill shoots up my back and I try to scream but still nothing escapes my lips.

I force myself to concentrate. I slow my breathing and stop struggling. My body lies still, limp. I close my eyes and take in a deep breath, fighting back against the urge to let panic plant its root.

A heartbeat later, I flash my eyes open. In the corner, something familiar lurks among the fog. I squint, barely able to see the object in my peripheral vision. I sigh. It's my desk. I'm in my room. The weight on my stomach intensifies as the dark sinews start to move from the ceiling and down the walls. I have to remind myself to stay calm again, to gather my wits, force myself to steady my breaths despite the encroaching darkness.

As my breathing steadies, a noise reaches my ears. It's unsteady, almost rhythmic, but too disorganized to be music or an orchestrated sound. I search the room for its source, and my eyes settle on the constant pulse of the fog. Panic and confusion override my curiosity as I listen, shaking. It's emitting a steady thrum, a low throb. The fog is making the noise.

As it travels slowly, inch by inch at a snail's pace, the space between the sinuous fibers seems to open, to stretch out. It's almost like the beating of a heart except there doesn't seem to be a rhythm about it. My brow further wrinkles as I catch sight of something new behind the fog. Each time it separates, a deep crimson red reveals itself. It's not a solid color, more like thick stuttered paint strokes. No. It's something else, not like paint, there is a form. I squint between pulses, the red strokes revealing themselves then going back into hiding behind the thick fog.

My eyes go wide as the form of the crimson comes into view more fully. Handprints smear down the wall, like someone had tried to crawl up the wall with bloodied hands. But from what? My body goes cold. I want to wrench back, ball up and tuck my legs behind my arms and close my eyes. But my body isn't listening to me. I could close my eyes, but just as the thought enters my mind, I hear it.

Click. Click.

My eyes shoot from corner to corner. I don't know which direction it came from, and I can't see anything beyond the thick fog-drenched walls. Lying flat on my back, I can only see about four feet down the wall below the ceiling. The fog pulses quicker, like the steady beat of the drum building to some magnificent finale. The red streaks are harder to make out behind the openings as the black tendrils drop past my field of view, creeping ever closer.

It feels like forever, lying helpless on my back, unable to move, petrified. I will my legs to carry me, sprint me away from the terror inching ever closer. But my body conspires against me. It's like a guillotine, holding me back, just waiting for the blade to fall.

Click. Click. Click.

Before I can dart my eyes to the right, something appears, much too close for comfort, below my feet. At first, it's just a black spot against the window blinds where the fog chokes out any hint of outside light. My pupils manage to focus and there *it* is. Pitch black, a mass of exposed ebony muscle pulses over long slender bones, a mist hovering about it make its features appear recessed and sunken.

I jerk back, at least I try. I stutter out a breath and beg my body to move, to crawl backwards up my bed. I want so badly to press my body against the cherry wood headboard, to cower, yes, cower at the top of the bed and wish away what I see before my eyes.

It just stands there, motionless, only its head visible at the edge of my vision. Its stare is intense, digging into me, boring into my very being. Those black holes. No, there is color. A dark, dark crimson that matches the hand smears on the wall.

Click. Click.

Suddenly it's gone, vanished. I swallow. Where did it go? I search the top half of the room, the only places I can see as my body lays flat, face up, on the bed beyond my control.

Click. Click.

I hear it again, but I still can't see it. I fight to control my breathing, to force myself to calm down. It's still there, somewhere in the dark, I know it's there. Without warning, the fog begins to pulse quicker. Its tendrils begin to writhe along a wider path, revealing even more smears along the wall. There are so many bloody hands smeared along the wall.

I catch something soaring through the air before I can make any sense of it. I try to cover my face as my computer chair slams against the ceiling and tumbles back down, ricocheting against the foot of my bed, barely missing my feet, before crashing to the floor and out of sight. My body shakes as the bed rocks. I try to move, to utilize the movement to get myself in motion, trying to kick-start my stalled caboose, away from whatever lurks in the shadows. Then the creature dashes across my vision. Its ebony neck jerks as it flies across my view and then disappears again. I freeze my attempts to get mobile.

The sound of the air being shoved from my chest and then dragged back in mighty gulps echoes in my head. I close my eyes, trying to ignore the thing I know is present in the room with me. Adrenaline pumps through my veins, but I have no way of utilizing it, no way to let it carry me away and off to safety. I want to scream, to bellow out all the bottled-up fear that pounds in my chest.

My mind screeches to a halt as something touches my stomach atop the thick comforter. The touch is light at first, but the pressure grows, bearing down on my midsection. I squint in pain as the thing, the hand, whatever it is, presses down and then suddenly lightens and slides up to my chest. I can't see it but I know it's there.

Then it is gone like a flash of light, like it had never existed at all. With a slow delicacy my eyes creep open, horrified at what I might find, but unable to remain fixed behind their shades, a conflicting mix of curiosity and fear tearing at my mind. The pulse of the fog slows. The crimson prints and smears laugh at me as they're devoured and reborn again and again. They are everywhere, like a hundred hands thrashing out from the grave, screaming their penance from hell, begging for only a momentary reprieve from the flames that lick their hides.

I shift my eyes from side to side, searching for the figure again, whatever it was, or wasn't. I swear I feel my pointer finger move, but if it did it was useless. I can't look far enough down to verify, but I swear it moved. I let out a breath, then, as if on cue, everything goes silent. The deep throbbing of the fog stops, replaced by silence.

A warm breath mists my right ear. I freeze, mind and body stuck in the same hellish paralysis. I beg to bury myself into oblivion, squeezing shut my horrified eyes.

"Not yet," a whisper growls in my ear.

As if some command had bid it, the fog vanishes, revealing the bland shadow-cast walls of my room. Light filters in from the window to my right and the ceiling returns to its natural dull brown. I force a deep breath between my lips in relief. A ray of hope appears as I manage to move my arm, then my feet. Unwilling to be pressed flat against my mattress any longer, and still uneasy from the paralysis, I burst up and out of the bed.

I swivel my head back and forth, scanning the room, searching for whatever had spoken into my ear. There is nothing. Just a pile of clothes in the corner and the small dresser that holds more of my clothes. In the other corner my computer chair sits upright by my desk, right where it had been when I fell asleep. It *had* just been a dream, another damn night terror.

It's not your first rodeo, Taren. Calm down.

My body shakes, releasing the adrenaline that still courses through my veins. I feel so stupid, pathetic. I'm an adult, but still my dreams wreak havoc on me. Sure, they're different, they're more like hallucinations, but they're still just dreams.

I crawl back up onto the bed, my back against the headboard. I lower my head in defeat. Why does this have to happen, why do I have to be plagued by the imaginary? I dam up the sobs that are building up behind my eyes, but it's useless. No one else can see me right now so I let them break.

"What the hell is wrong with me?"

5

I hate doctors' offices.

It's not the doctors, at least not exactly. It's the waiting room really. Of course, that's where I sit now, a waiting room.

The waiting room at the UNC Hospital Neuroscience Clinic isn't particularly horrible, but it's still a doctor's office. I don't know exactly what it is I hate about them so much, but there's just something about them. Maybe it's the waiting in general, or maybe it's seeing the less fortunate patients sitting around in their various states of health. It makes me feel selfish being there, maybe even a little paranoid at times.

My "problem" only affects me at night, out of sight from curious eyes. Sometimes I daydream about it happening during the day, in class. I can see me stuck at a desk, eyes darting, body slumped over on the plastic table-top, and suddenly I jump up screaming about something horrifying in the room. Most of the class would understand, it wouldn't be the first time I'd fallen asleep during class courtesy of my narcolepsy.

Sure, it's terrifying and it's kept me awake many a night, but compared to some of the people, the shells I've witnessed in this very same waiting room over the past year, my problem seems so small, so insignificant.

This early in the morning the waiting room is relatively empty, except for the older man two chairs over from me. Of all the chairs, twelve to be exact in the thoughtfully furnished and decorated room, of course he chose to sit right next to me. I lean to the side again, trying to move farther away from the old man. I don't have a problem with people, but really?

I lift my phone and check my Facebook feed. More nothing, no one posts anything interesting this early. I notice the old man leaning toward me, eyeing my phone, but before I can pocket it, the thick mahogany door crafted into the opposite wall creaks open and a nurse steps into the waiting room. She calls my name and smiles, which comes as a surprise for reasons unknown even to myself.

"Taren Evans," the nurse says, a wide smile across her thin jaw line. It's Vickie again.

She's much too happy for this early in the morning. I rise, glad to have a reason to abscond away from the old man and get my personal space back.

I give Vickie my best morning smile as I walk up. It isn't that great.

"Morning." I try to sound cheery.

"Good morning, Mr. Evans," Vickie chimes back with an amused grin, her eyes too alert and bright. She turns and leads me down the narrow corridor and into the guts of the clinic. "You're not much of a morning person, are you?"

Is it that obvious? I straighten my back. I really do need to get more sleep.

"Nah, not exactly," I admit, toning down how much I truly despise mornings. I think she gets the point though.

Vickie steps back and waves me through the open door.

"Here we are."

I nod and squeeze by Vickie. I hold my expression as I blush inside after my arm brushes against her chest. I try to act like nothing happened. Flustered, I take a seat next to the typical doctor's office bed, the one with the sheet of paper wrapped around it, opting to keep my feet on the ground. Even at five eleven, my feet dangle aimlessly in the air when the doctor makes me sit at that blame bed's edge. I prefer a standard chair any day.

As I sit, Vickie rattles off the usual series of questions. Have I traveled outside of the country? No. Do I have any allergies? How many times do they really need to ask that question, I'm pretty sure it hasn't changed since I was here two days ago. Am I sexually active? I can't help but grin. I know it's immature, but really? It depends on how you define active, I guess.

After a few more questions and a freezing cold stethoscope, Vickie informs me that the doctor will be in soon, which usually translates to give him at least twenty minutes. She shuts the door behind her and I pull out my phone, hoping for something to entertain myself with, or to avoid the thought of my night terrors as long as I can. I bypass the usual social networks in favor of some news.

I scroll through the feed, passing one useless story after another. I don't give a shit what rude comment President Trump tweeted and I couldn't care less who Kim Kardashian is sleeping with now. The only interesting story is about some meth lab bust at a mall in the western part of the state. That's an accomplishment if you ask me. A meth lab. In a mall. Really?

A knock on the door forces me to give up on the news. Startled, I watch the door crack open. Dr. Gillespie slips in and closes the door behind him. He's an intelligent looking man, which suits him as a neuroscientist. His thick, light brown hair slopes up high above his forehead and then tumbles down just above his right ear, eventually connecting to a full beard and mustache that make him appear older than I think he really is. I have him pegged at mid-forties, but I'm not about to ask.

His steel blue eyes peer at me thoughtfully, looking me over from head to toe, probably guessing why I chose the chair over the bed. I must admit that it unnerves me, though I refuse to show it. He doesn't mean any harm, I'm sure of it. Despite his gaze, I know he's a kind man, stern and stoic at times, but kind. I mean the man gives out his personal number to patients.

"Good morning, Taren," he nearly whispers, reaching out his hand which I accept. His voice is coarse but kind, a quiet tenor that bodes well in his line of work.

"Morning, doc," I reply, sinking back into my seat, ready to find out what Gillespie has for me.

"So how was your weekend?" the doctor asks, resting a manila folder on his lap.

"Nothing special." I shrug. "Just watched some TV shows basically."

"Sounds good to me. I've not had the time to watch my shows lately. Oh well, enough about me. I'd like to start out with your sleep study results," Dr. Gillespie begins. He takes a seat on the chair opposite to me and opens the manila folder he had tucked under his arm. He scans whatever information is in the folder thoughtfully.

"I'm glad we were finally able to get one of your episodes on record, Taren." Gillespie shuffles in his chair. "I've started going through the readings but I haven't had the chance to look over the actual video feed yet. I'll get to it soon. However, it's fairly obvious you were experiencing a terror though. You had a significant increase in heart-rate and brain activity, among other indicators."

Seriously? You've not even watched the video yet?

I grin and straighten in my chair, trying to not to show my displeasure.

He knows what he's doing, Taren. Calm it.

I sit back and listen as Gillespie explains more about what the study has uncovered, something about the periaqueductal gray of my brain and cortisol. I did understand the part about my adrenaline levels increasing though. I might be a psychology major at the university, but I have a way to go before I understand half of what he said about my brain.

Minutes later, Dr. Gillespie begins to wind down from his explanations.

"You're currently on Wellbutrin, right?" He cocks his head to the side.

"Yes." I've been on the antidepressant for several years now, I'm sure my folder says as much.

"I think the next step we should take now that we've had a better look at your sleep paralysis is to scale back a bit on the prescription. I'm going to write you a new prescription at a lower dosage," he explains. "I'm thinking that's at least part of the puzzle. One of its side effects is hallucinations and insomnia, and while with your narcolepsy it usually helps to assuage the attacks, the dosage may not be right for your specific combination of narcolepsy and sleep paralysis."

I nod even though it makes little sense to me. The damn drug *causes* hallucinations and insomnia, I already have plenty of those. But what do I know, they say it works.

Yes, I have mild narcolepsy, and yes, it's a horrible combination. When I was first put on the antidepressant to deal with some other issues it gave me headaches, but they soon wore off and ended altogether after my psychologist got the dosage right. When my sleep paralysis surfaced though, they had to tweak the dosage again, but it didn't seem to help.

"Are you sure that'll work? I mean didn't we change the dosage right at the beginning?" I ask, dragging the edge of my lip upward in a questioning gesture.

"We did," he agrees, drawing a finger along the file in his hand. "But, we increased it, hoping that an increased dosage might help. I'm thinking lowering below the original level might have actually been the better course of action."

I shrug, though I'm livid inside. Maybe I should get a second opinion. Looks like we'll be messing with that dosage again though in the meantime. Something tells me it won't be the last time either. Wonderful, but if it helps keep me asleep and keep the night terrors away, I'm all for it.

"Okay." It's all I manage.

"If nothing else I hope it will reduce the frequency of your episodes, Taren. At least while we pin down the real culprit. Does that sound okay?" Gillespie asks.

"I believe so, Dr. Gillespie." I nod again.

"All right then, I'll write out your new prescription," he explains as he gets to his feet, tucks the folder back under his right arm and plants his other hand on the door knob, "and I'll have Vickie show you the way out. They'll make your next appointment up front."

I nod again. Gillespie looks down and licks his lips absently before meeting my eyes again.

"One week." It was a bit abrupt but I sit still, amused inside but refusing to show it. "I'll have them set you up for an appointment sometime early next week so we can see how the new dosage is doing. I should have time to review your sleep study video by then. I'll see you then."

His hands both occupied, Gillespie salutes me with the folder like I'm some kid. I nod, not knowing what else to do as he leaves me alone in the small room, shutting the door behind him. I release a breath and force a smile. We're getting somewhere at least, I think.

I know the way out, but I wait anyway. I think I'm supposed to.

6

I lived through another episode last night.

The fog, then the dark figure darting about, standing ominously in the corner, and then disappearing. I hate it. I hate it so fucking much. How the hell can this be my *normal*? At least it never touches me. Maybe it can't. I hope it can't.

All I want is to go a week, two weeks, a month, hell maybe even a year, without a night terror. If it was just a normal dream, even a normal nightmare, I'd be all right with it. I could deal with that like normal people, separate the dream world with the real world. But this? No. When it happens, my real world is literally merged with the dream world like some movie or messed up story.

It's beyond horrifying and it wreaks havoc on my sleep and my bed. I've went through more sweat-soaked sheets than anyone should have to. And my narcolepsy, mild as it is, being afraid to close your eyes for fear of them literally opening in a dream that's just as real as my hand in front of my face, just makes it worse. The skin around my eyes make my fatigue evident with their graying circles.

I pop my reduced dosage prescription and step out of the bathroom I share with Asher and tip-toe down the fake hardwood floor. Matt is still asleep, and just about anything wakes him. Unlike Matt though, I have an eleven am chemistry class in Kenan Building. I squeeze my eyes shut and rub vigorously at my tired lids, trying to replace the image of the figure in my night terrors with Morgan's gentle brown eyes. As usual, it doesn't work. Instead I just try to ignore the visions.

Rounding the corner, I gather a bowl and spoon, pour a heaping pile of Frosted Flakes, and take care not to spill my milk as I take a seat on the couch. I flip on the television and absentmindedly scroll through the channels before giving up and turning on Netflix. Hundreds, maybe thousands of shows, and I can't concentrate enough to care about any of them. I continue to scroll.

Before I can select something to watch, the front door swings open and Rohan strolls in and lets the door slam shut behind him. The bang rings in my head, it's still too early. I grimace, hoping it didn't wake Matt, I don't need to deal with an angry Matt this early.

"Morning, Taren," Rohan greets me, only a slight hint of his Indian heritage hiding behind his unusual southern accent. I guess that's what happens when your family immigrates from India to America over two generations back. His brown skin is perfectly smooth and he has a headful of dark black hair that would make any balding man jealous. From the looks of his dad, who visits campus often, he's in no danger of ever losing his thick covering.

"Morning." I look up just long enough to acknowledge him and let him know he shut the door much too loudly. He's dressed casually in a pair of blue jeans and a white graphic t-shirt, today's variety reads "If I'm not on a watch list, someone isn't doing their job" with a big set of binoculars on them. I don't know where the hell he gets those shirts but I must admit, some of them are funny.

"So, we talked about Alan Turing in my IT Security class this morning," Rohan says as he deposits his backpack on the floor next to the couch and enters the kitchen. There's a brief silence. I'm not sure if I'm supposed to respond or what.

"You know who that is, right?" he asks, leaning around the corner, eying me eagerly.

"Alan Turing? No idea," I say matter-of-factly.

"Seriously?" Rohan asks. The sound of the refrigerator door closing and a soda fizzing up accompanies his sarcastic and accusing tone.

"Yeah, seriously," I confirm. "I mean the name sounds familiar but only faintly."

"He's the father of modern computer science. The guy who cracked the Germans' enigma code in World War II." Rohan stops and looks at me again, obviously expecting the light to click in my head. It doesn't. He stands in front of me with a clear glass full of soda now. "He's British, like *you*. Don't they teach you about him over there?"

"Oh! So, since I'm *British*, I should know about him," I reply, letting the sarcasm roll off my tongue, putting up air quotes as the word *British* escaped my lips. I smile and shake my head. "First, and for the nth time, I'm not British, I'm Welsh. *Big* difference."

"Yeah, yeah. Same kingdom." Rohan dismisses it with a grin. It's a common routine. I can't tell for sure whether he just keeps forgetting or if he just likes nagging me about it. It doesn't matter, it's all in good fun either way.

"Whatever," I joke back, doubling up my weak Welsh accent. "It's not like I lived there long enough. I mean we moved to the states when I was fourteen. Maybe I missed the 'Essential Alan Turing' class over in Wales."

I put my hands down after another set of air quotes and scoop a spoonful of Frosted Flakes.

"That's fair I guess," Rohan admits with a large grin and returns to the kitchen, probably to finish preparing his lunch.

I shake my head and retrieve my phone from my pocket to check the time. *10:25am*. Dammit. I'm going to be late for class again.

7

I take it to the edge, I do it till it bleeds, I push it to the limit, I ain't ever gonna sleep.

I let the lyrics finish before I depress the start button, killing the engine. I could listen to Never Say Die on repeat for days, but I have to get out of the car sometime tonight.

It's getting dark, but the sun still paints the complex in a golden hue. Its rays leave a faint glow on the parking lot and sends long shadows across the short lawns. I enter the dorm hall and hitch a ride on the elevator up to the second floor. The doors open and I'm walking down the hall.

Ahead of me, standing in front of my dorm room is Morgan, as planned. It's movie night.

I straighten my stance and let an excited shiver take its course down my spine. Her jeans are so tight tonight and fortunately for me she's facing away, distracted by her phone. I savor the sight as I shuffle up behind her without a sound before grabbing her butt.

She jumps, about throws her phone across the hallway and exhales a high-pitched yelp before catching sight of me. I'm all grins, but I refuse to give her time to react, I don't much like the idea of getting slapped. Instead I wrap an arm around her back and I go in for the kill. My lips press against hers and she surrenders to me. Strawberry again.

"All right," Morgan says after pushing me back. "That's enough. What do you think you're doing coming up behind me like that and…" she pauses, looking around the hall like it's something horrible to say, "…pinching me like that."

"I was just thinking I wanted some of that—" Before I can finish my sentence, Morgan seals my lips with a firmly placed finger. I let a grin stretch across my face.

"Right. Let's go inside." Morgan's lips stay in a funny pout, hiding a grin of her own.

I unlock the door and follow her inside, flipping on the light switch. No one else is home. Matt's still in class, Rohan's at work and Asher…I don't have a clue.

Inside Morgan drops back onto the stiff college dorm sofa, leaning her head back and stretching out her arms. I can't help but grin again as I saunter by.

"I'm going to put away my stuff," I say, passing the couch. "Go ahead and pick out a movie."

She bites her lip, which sends a chill up my spine. How the hell is that so sexy? I shake my head and leave her in the living area. A few steps later and I'm in my small bedroom. I throw my worn backpack on the floor and kick off my shoes. I roughly place the Nikes at the foot of my bed with my other shoes and go back to my desk and dump my pockets.

I slip out of the bedroom and find Morgan still leaning back on the couch, scrolling through a list of movies on the television.

"So, you picked something out yet?" I ask, diverting my path into the kitchen. "You want anything to drink?"

"Uh…I've got it narrowed down to three choices, maybe you can decide," she almost whispers, her voice silky and smooth.

"Okay," I respond, and then emphasize my next words which were obviously missed last time. "Want anything to drink?"

"Oh, yeah. I take it you don't have any tea?" Morgan bends her neck around and peers at me over the kitchen counter.

"Right you are." My roommates and I are quite content with buying whatever drink we need from the grocery store rather than making our own, and none of their teas do it for us anyway. "Unless of course you're volunteering to make some of your *awesome* sweet tea?"

"Right," she almost whispers with a feigned frown. "Nah, I'll pass. How about a Dr. Pepper? I'm positive you'll have that."

What can I say? She knows me. Well. I retrieve the soda from the fridge and pour two glasses before rounding the couch and plopping down on the couch up close to Morgan. I hand her a glass and take a sip out of my own. A small amethyst hangs below her neck, the necklace I gave her two days ago celebrating one year of her putting up with me.

"So, what do you got for us?" I ask.

"I don't know." Morgan shrugs, a confused look drawing across her face. "Nothing looks particularly great right now."

"You don't want to watch Star Trek again?" I ask, knowing the answer way before the words exit my lips.

"No!" she retorts with a note of finality.

"Yeah, I didn't think so." I guess not everyone loves Star Trek, Morgan sure doesn't. It must be her one flaw. "How about that show about the virus down in…uh…"

I raise my hand and wiggle it in front of me, trying to remember where the fictional story took place.

"Atlanta?" Morgan murmurs, unsure.

"Yes! That's it", I agree. "That's the one. Can't remember what it's called but that one."

"Ah, I don't know." Her voice is reserved. "I like it and all, but…"

"Maybe we should just skip the movie," I suggest. I know what I really want, but I know better. There are a few board games up in the hall closet and a deck of cards and a PlayStation under the television. Morgan's not much of a gamer though, and I can't say I am either.

"I can go for that, nothing sounds that great right now." Morgan repositions herself on the couch, bringing her body next to mine. I take in a small breath as her bare leg brushes against me.

"So, what do you want to do?" I ask.

"I don't know," she replies.

Half an hour of idle chatter passes. Morgan reminds me that she's going to Charlotte next month for the Starset and Bad Omens' concert with her older brother. I'd been invited but I couldn't manage to get off work in time. Oh, the joys of a part-time weekend job to get you through college. It's not the first concert I've missed and I'm sure it won't the last.

I tell her about my upcoming family reunion in Wales at the beginning of the coming year. How I want her to go with me, meet some more of my family and give me a reason to ignore some of the others. She giggles at that and her eyes light up at the thought of going to the United Kingdom.

"So, did you ever finish that philosophy paper? What was it about? Kant or something?"

"Yeah, it's supposed to be about the differences between Kant and Mill, but no, I've not finished it yet." I paint a large grin across my face, "I've barely started actually."

"Isn't it due like next week?" Morgan crinkles her brow and digs her eyes into me.

"Yeah, but I always do my best work at the last minute." It's true. I always do my best work under pressure.

"I'd flunk every paper I wrote if I tried that," Morgan laments. "Oh, how I hate writing papers."

"I just work better like that, that's all."

A few minutes pass of more-or-less boring idle chatter, still unable to settle on something to watch and too chivalrous to make a move. After a while, Morgan lays her head on my shoulder. I gently place my head atop hers and let out a sigh.

"So, have you had any more night terrors since your doctor

changed your prescription?" Morgan asks, snuggling up closer, her nose snuggling on my neck.

I can hear the apprehension in her voice. She knows I'm not exactly fond of talking about it, my night terrors. We're both looking forward toward the blank television screen, staring into nothing. I tip the edge of my lip, but quickly try to hide it behind a half grin.

"Yeah." I squint. "Two days ago."

There is a worry in her amber eyes, something deep and caring. She lifts her head and peers at me, her face close to mine.

"Why didn't you tell me before?" she asks.

"I don't know," I start, unsure what to say. It's stupid to hold it all in, but that's me. "I figured why bother you with it."

She lifts her hand and places her palm on my cheek, caressing my face like a mother cradling a newborn until her hand comes to a rest on my neck. A chill travels down my body at her touch. Her hands are so smooth, and her deep brown eyes are caring as she gazes like I'm broken; like she can fix me.

"It's okay. I want you to tell me." Morgan scoots a little closer, pressing our sides together. I can feel her chest against me. I stare into her eyes. "Do you think it's getting better?"

"It's hard to tell," I huff, wanting to tell her that anything would be better with her this close, but I don't. "Maybe, maybe not. I won't know for a few days at least."

She forces a grin. The gentleness behind her eyes tells me that she cares, that she wants the best for me. I love her, but how can I put her through my problems? It'd be cruel of me to expect her to stay with me through all the sleepless nights. *Wouldn't it?*

"So, are you going to be all right without me this weekend?" Morgan asks, not an ounce of sarcasm in her voice. She leaves in the morning for Charleston, SC, to go back down to her parents' house for her mom's birthday.

"I'll be fine." For some reason my defenses rise at her question. "I might have night terrors but I'm not a kid."

It comes out angrier than I'd meant it to. I wince and look at Morgan.

"I'm sorry, I didn't mean to sound mean." My voice softens as I try to convey my thoughts. "But I'll be fine, I've got the guys here if nothing else."

"Yeah." She grins, slipping a hand onto my chest. "But they can't take your mind off it like I can…can they?"

Morgan feigns worry and bites her lip again. I take in a deep breath as she props her forehead against my own.

"No. No, they can't." I feel her breath on my lips and it's all I can do not to push forward and press my lips against hers.

"I love you, Taren," she says breathlessly.

That's it, I lean forward, pressing my lips against hers. I taste her lips as my mouth opens and she follows along. Everything around me fades as every sensation courses through me. Longing. Desire. Love. Passion.

I reach around and take hold of her waist as she angles around and straddles me, slipping a hand under my shirt. It doesn't take long for me to wrap a hand around her back while the other reaches for her neck, cradling her in my palms, pulling her to me. I want her so badly as I pull her body fully against mine, feeling every inch of her form against my chest.

"Woah!" a voice shouts from the doorway. "I like a good show and all, but I don't want to see Taren."

Morgan jumps off my lap and back onto the couch. I glare up at Matt who has apparently just gotten back from class. Next to him is Asher, grinning from ear to ear.

"Dude! What the hell? What are you two doing back already?" I know it's a stupid question, but between my burning red cheeks, heavy breaths and frazzled mental state, it's the best I can come up with. Next to me Morgan is staring at the ground, biting her lip nervously.

"Uh…I always get back at about eight," Matt replies, still smirking. "Nothing new here."

"We're out!" Asher shoves Matt toward the door. "Forgot we've got other *stuff* to do."

Matt wrinkles his brow at Asher and grins, dropping back a step closer to the door.

"No, no, Asher. It's okay." I fight off the embarrassment. It'll just have to wait I guess.

"If you two want, I'm sure we can go to our rooms, if that'll…" Asher tries again.

"Nah."

8

I'm sitting in the waiting room at the neuroscience clinic again, thankful that no one's decided to take up residence right beside me, yet. It's Tuesday and despite my worries, I've been episode free for a full week. It's not the longest I've gone between episodes but that's so much better than the last year. It's been a breath of a fresh air.

It's definitely helped my outlook. I still get anxious at night going to bed, but it's nothing like the nearly crippling worry that kept me awake just weeks ago. I'm not horrified to close my eyes at night, wishing I can just stay awake all night and avoid sleep altogether. It's been a good week. Plus, Morgan came back from Charleston early yesterday morning and we made up for Matt and Asher's little interruption on Friday.

I've only just arrived at the clinic but I already hate sitting in the waiting room, as usual. This early in the morning there's nothing much to see on the social networks, so I'm flipping through a Car & Driver magazine that the staff left on one of the many end tables. As I leaf through the pages my mind just keeps saying, "Nope, never going to happen, Taren" or "It's only two hundred grand. Right!"

An older couple sit across from me. Their faces wrinkled with age, feeble fingers interlaced together occasionally exchanging an affectionate grin. I can't help but smile inside. I drop my gaze back to the magazine. A new Aston Martin, probably the next Bond car, selling for just two hundred and sixty grand. Yeah, I'll be stuck in my Honda for a long time.

In the background, I can hear the receptionist taking calls and tapping at a keyboard, one slow key at a time. It's like water torture, each click of the keys another continuous drip. It's all overlaid by the quiet hum of an air conditioning unit keeping the building at an acceptable temperature. It's a hot one today. Thank God for A/C, but I think they might have gotten a little too excited. It can't be above sixty-five in here. The large LED TV plays the morning news in silence with subtitles appearing and disappearing at the bottom of the screen. It's larger than I'd normally expect at a doctor's office. It gives me visions of Dr. Gillespie or one of his co-workers shifting the furniture around at night and hosting a company movie party or something.

The door chime dings gently and a mom and her son enter and check in. Before they can take a seat a few chairs over, I drop the *Car & Driver* magazine I'm reading into the seat next to me and pick up another random magazine.

Damn, I hope that didn't look as rude as it was.

She's a young mother, probably mid to late twenties, shoulder length blonde hair, soft jaw, overall attractive. Her boy's a scrawny little thing, I'd say about six to nine years old maybe, dressed in a Spiderman t-shirt and khaki shorts that make his legs look like pencils.

Flashes of sky on the giant screen steal my attention from Pencil-legs. Good, they're showing the weather. Ugh, maybe not so good. Looks like the heat isn't going away anytime soon. Mid-nineties might not be much to someone down in Florida or Texas, but here in North Carolina, even though we routinely endure all four seasons within one week or even one day, it just downright hot. Living in Wales for the first fourteen years of my life didn't help, even North Carolina seems too hot.

Canada sounds pretty good. But would Morgan follow me to Canada, maybe New England?

The weather vanishes from the screen and a commercial starts up. Apparently, people who care about the weather also need to know that the channel will be airing the second Transformers movie tonight at eight. I drop my eyes to my feet and ride along reluctantly as my mind takes me back to Wales when I was just eleven. It was one of the first movies that Iestyn, my older brother, took me to, a midnight showing at that. Yeah, they don't do those anymore it seems. Instead they just release them the day before the release date. It's stupid if you ask me. The midnight showing just felt cool, but oh well.

I remember standing in line in the cinema for the first showing. It was huge, starting up at the ticket line and lining the wall all the way out the door. I was excited just like Iestyn. I might have been a little hyped up on sugar from our late-night candy binge before we left for the movie though. If I remember right, I was wearing an old-school Optimus Prime t-shirt and he had on a Bumblebee tee. His hair was dark, almost as black as mine, but his eyes where pale green. I remember he was excited about starting his last year of high school and then going off to college eventually.

That was the last movie he ever took me to. He'd never finish the school year, or attend college. He'd never get married, anything. A few months later a drunk driver t-boned him on St. Mary Street in Cardiff. The police said he died instantly.

"Taren Evans." A voice shatters the vision, tearing me away from the memory. I snap back and eye the unfamiliar nurse waiting for me. No Vickie today it seems. I get up and moments later I'm sitting in another sterile patient room waiting for Dr. Gillespie.

My thoughts drift back to Iestyn. I miss him. He would've loved the states. My mom and dad didn't move us from Wales over to the US until I was fourteen, but I really think Iestyn would have enjoyed it here. I find myself asking why, often. Why did he have to go? Why did that asshole have to get drunk and behind the wheel of a car? Why my brother? There are no answers, but it doesn't stop me from asking.

I stare at the empty silver sink basin, the simple boxes of sterile rubber gloves, and the black plastic thermometer guards. It all appears drearier than usual. I grit my teeth and dig my eyes into the floor. I let out a deep breath.

It was a long time ago. Move on, Taren. The words swirl around my mind.

A loud knock shocks me from my stupor, or maybe it was just a knock. Yeah, just a knock. It inches open and Dr. Gillespie wedges through. He smiles, his blue eyes seem kinder than the last time I was here. I guess I'm getting used to him finally.

"Good morning, Taren." Gillespie extends his hand.

"Morning, doctor." I accept his outstretched hand and give it a good shake. His grip is firm as usual.

The doctor takes a seat opposite me and leans back against the wall, throwing a leg up to prop his folder on.

"So," he begins. "How have you been?"

"Great." I focus on how great it's felt the past week to go to bed and have a full night's sleep, uninterrupted by untold horrors.

"Really?" Dr. Gillespie asks, forming his lips into a wry smile.

"Well, yes. I mean…" I stutter. It's true, the last week has been great, but maybe I shouldn't get too excited just yet. I don't want the doctor thinking I don't need his help anymore. "Yes, I've been good. I think your new prescription is doing the trick. But it's only been a week."

The doctor leans forward to reposition himself in his chair.

"Good," he says. "So, have you had any episodes since we reduced your dosages? Fewer maybe?"

"Well, at first I actually thought it was going to get worse. The very night I started the new dosage I had another episode." But I'm quick to clarify. "But it wasn't any worse than any I've had before, it just happened to happen that night I guess. I've not had one since that though. That'll be one week tonight. So yeah, I think it's working."

The doctor nods, his eyes never leaving me. "That sounds good. Maybe even progress."

"Yeah, I think it is."

Dr. Gillespie finally breaks his stare and looks down at the folder in his lap. He fingers through a few pages and lets out a monster sigh, crinkling his brow.

"Is everything okay?" I ask. He looks like he's about to give me the bad news. It unnerves me.

"Oh, yes. Everything's fine." He assures me, smiling to dissuade any misgiving I might have. "I was just taking a glance at your file. I watched your sleep study."

I lean forward.

"Everything seems to be consistent with my previous findings with your vitals during the study. It's obvious it was sleep paralysis with how your vitals spiked despite your body being immobile."

He leans forward and his expression relaxes.

"Just remember that your experience so far is limited. It's only been a week. We know that lowering your dosage is just a step, it won't stop your episodes. They will come back." Gillespie drags a hand through his thick hair. "We're just attempting to reduce the frequency of the attacks right now and hopefully reduce the longevity of each episode."

My antidepressant has been a life-saver ever since my brother's...accident. But at the same time, it seems they've been part of the problem, too. I hope we'll know for certain soon.

"Okay. How well do you think it'll work?" I ask, hoping for good news.

"I can't really say, but considering what you've said already: One week episode free, right?" He watches me expectantly with his steely blues. I simply nod. "I'm hopeful. Maybe we can spread them out, make them more of a monthly or semi-monthly occurrence. It's better than what you've been through, Taren."

"It is." I sigh. I knew I wasn't looking at a cure. I knew it before I ever came to my appointment today, but for some reason I always feel like the doctor will come into the room and tell me in an excited voice that they found a way to stop the sleep paralysis, to cure me.

Dr. Gillespie sits back in his chair and straightens.

"I also have to warn you that it could get worse, too. This could simply be a good week." His positive demeanor drops, a genuine sadness glowering behind his eyes. "There are a lot of variables, a lot of unknowns."

"I know," I say, taken aback to the cold reality of my disorder.

"But we're going to get there, we'll keep trying."

I smile. It's mostly a false grin, a façade to cover the disappointment and dread roiling around in my gut. But, it's also genuine. There's no doubt that Dr. Gillespie's on my side. Well, he has to be, I'm paying him. Well, my insurance is at least.

This isn't the end. It's only the beginning.

9

The cursor blinks on the screen. It hasn't moved more than inch in the past five minutes without being backspaced back to its starting point.

I stare at the glowing surface, millions of tiny pixels screaming back at me, burning into my eyes. My eyes are watering, begging, weeping for sleep. But I have a paper to finish that's due tomorrow. I definitely underestimated this one. Typing out five pages on the differences in the ethical philosophies of Immanuel Kant and John Stuart Mill just isn't coming to me like I'd planned.

I shouldn't have waited this long, letting my procrastination form a noose around my neck. I know better than trying to stay up this late, though most wouldn't call ten late. At least not most college students. It's one of the limitations of my narcolepsy. My meds keep me alert most of the day, but night still takes its toll.

My fingers do a slow dance across the keyboard, spitting a few labored words onto the screen. Immediately I erase them, pursing my lips, and trying to shake myself awake. Only another paragraph or two and I'll be done with this blasted paper. Five pages is five pages.

Come on, Taren. It's not that hard. It's Kant and Mill, you've got this.

Finally, my fingers find their momentum among the keys. Each key press is a dull thud, another noise to drown out the monotony of this report. Faster now, the letters fill the next row. It's the concluding paragraph, at least it better be.

I actually enjoy the philosophy, at least when I'm not a zombie. The battle of the wits and an undertaking to derive a consistent moral and ethical system. It's intriguing to say the least and Kant and Mill are no exception.

I snap back out of writing mode, wiping the drowsy tears from my eyes. I swear my eyes would drown me if it brought me sleep, even if only for a few hours. I take a generous gulp from the Dr. Pepper sitting on my desk. My eyes catch the bottom of my glass. Empty.

"Dammit!" That won't do, so I kick my chair back and stagger out into the hallway, taking my empty glass with me.

The dorm is mostly dark except for the shades of light-gray and hues of pale blue that filter through the window drapes and splash sporadically along the living room wall. The wooden floor is cold against my naked feet. Ahead, faint colors blink and flash along the wall in the living room. I round the bend and find Matt and Asher watching a movie. Asher waves, but neither of the boys say a thing as I enter the kitchen. I retrieve the bottle of Dr. Pepper from the fridge, guarding my eyes from the bright beams of light escaping the television, and pour another full glass of the amazing brown liquid.

I slip back quietly to my room, trying not to bother Matt and Asher, and take up my reluctant post behind my desk again. With another sip down the hatch, I start typing again. Twenty long minutes later and a ton of backspacing and rewriting, my caffeine-fueled paper is complete. I print off a copy and stuff it in my backpack.

"Done." I say the word like it's a mighty decree.

I snatch up my cup and guzzle down the remaining quarter of a glass and then drop it on the desk. Getting to my feet, I open my eyes wide, straining to keep myself awake just long enough to get to the bed.

Yeah, that can be hard with narcolepsy.

I slither my hands under my shirt and drag it over my head. I launch the shirt at the clothes bin but the floor generously accepts it instead. A few steps closer to the bed, I manage to unfasten and unzip my jeans. I let them fall to the ground, then scoop them up, barely avoiding a stumble to the floor, and toss them in the general direction of my shirt. *Damn, I suck at this.*

"Oh well," I reply to myself and an empty room, a sure sign I'm passing into sleep whether I want it or not. I collapse onto the bed. It's firm, but its warmth wraps around me, earning a contented sigh from my lips.

Before I can wrestle with the covers, I sense my eyelids growing heavier by the moment, lowering, pulling me away.

10

It's dark in my room, colder than I remember it being when I fell asleep. I let my eyes roam the room, trying to make out the shapes around me. Shades of gray cast in from the blinded window.

Oh no!

I realize I can't move. A chill runs up my spine as I realize it's happening again.

No, no, no, no. Not this. Anywhere but here. Anywhere but here.

I beg to move, to wake up.

I tremble as the charcoal fog sprouts from the ceiling above me. In slow pulses, it builds on the surface, emanating outward. The fear in my gut ratchets up a notch.

I will my arm to move, just an inch, just to feel it brush against my sheets, to remind it who the master is. I get nothing in return. Despite its stillness, I can feel my disobedient limb. I can feel it tingle, every inch of it, but I'm powerless to move it. The fog has reached the edge of the ceiling now, its ghastly black tendrils throbbing along the crown of the room. I can hear it now, that subtle but constant thrum. It's like a droning dull static going in and out of phase.

I want to sink into the mattress, but my wish goes unbidden. My eyes search the shadows below the ebony fog as far as they can reach without being able to move beyond my peripheral vision. Everything looks to be in place. Still the frigid air burdening down on my frame chills me to the bone. I don't remember it being like this before. I try to swallow but it's useless. For a moment, I fear I'll choke on my own saliva, but I remind myself that I'm okay.

Just calm down.

I'm helpless as the fog's tendrils commence their conquest of the walls. A patch of mist envelopes a photo of my family on the opposite wall, and then one of me and Iestyn. I want to clench my jaw in anger, but I can't. I can't even move my own mouth. I'm so *fucking* useless and scared. In my mind I'm clenching my fist, though I'm sure my hands haven't moved an inch, as anger builds inside me, layered in fear and the adrenaline that's shooting through my veins.

A deep guttural scream bursts through the walls. I jump, mortified by the howl. My breathing comes harder now though my chest sags in on itself, making it difficult. My eyes dart around the room. I can't tell which direction the scream came from, or if it came from within these walls. I take a long, labored breath before I hyperventilate.

Stuck in place, supine, I search the ceiling. Another scream bellows, piercing the darkness. I shudder.

Did that come from out in the hall? Is it coming for me?

It's never been like this before. I've never heard it howl like that, only whisper.

I clamp my eyes shut, refusing to look as a quiet creak reaches my ears. I freeze, knowing exactly what the sound is. The creak of door hinges confirms my fear. Something's coming.

The thrum of the fog pushing down the walls starts to beat in my mind. It's getting louder, like the beat of a drum against my eardrums, it bears down on me. My chest sinks under the pressure.

Above the throb, I detect the shuffle of feet over the hardwood floor of my bedroom. I keep my eyes closed, refusing to see whatever it is. I don't want to see it. I don't need to see it. It's just a nightmare, just a fucking nightmare.

Click. Click.

I can't do it anymore. I let my eyes burst open, the familiar sound tearing through my curiosity and fear, overriding my need to look away. For a moment, I keep my eyes steady on the ceiling, not moving. It's thick with the roiling fog. There are none of the usual crimson prints behind the undulating sinew. Just black, pure black. The color and texture of the ceiling has surrendered to whatever evil lies beyond the fog. But I refuse to surrender. I attempt to move again, and again, but my body refuses to respond.

After what feels like an eternity, I muster the courage to look down to chance seeing what I fully expect to be there. My eyes creep down the wall and I instantly want to wrench my eyes back to the ceiling, but I can't do it. My vision is glued to a blackened figure at the foot of my bed. It stands there, erect and upright, every glowering sinew of its body emanating a hellish desire as it stares me down. I shrink under its drilling eyes but somehow, I'm unable to unlock my gaze from those infernal orbs. Tonight, the creature is different, I don't know how, but I know it all the same.

Is it coming for me this time?

I curse myself for even thinking it, but still I can't snatch my eyes away from the creature. Even with its mouth closed I can see the rows of razor sharp fangs protruding from each lip.

The throb of the fog intensifies. It pounds against my body and skull. I squint under the pressure but refuse to take my eyes off the creature leering at the end of my bed, staring me down, sizing me up, planning something horrible that only it knows. The percussion of the fog grates against my skull. It's like a massive subwoofer at a metal concert is set next to my head, hammering out a deep bass note with each thrum of the fog, directly into my ear.

I want to scream, to escape this paralytic prison. The pain in my head is searing. I clamp my eyes closed, trying to drown out the noises in my own thoughts, daring to look away from the thing at my feet. I know that the noise is just in my head, but it doesn't matter as it beats against my skull. My ears throb with every thump. I know the creature is still watching me, still standing ominously at the foot my bed, but I refuse to open my eyes. Then somehow, above the beat I hear it.

Click. Click.

I force my eyes open, my eyelids pulsing with each pounding blow of the bass.

It's gone.

I search the room, only able to see the top half of the room surrounding me, though it's canvased in thick ebony fog.

Where is it? Where'd it go?

Click. Click.

The noise seeps into my ears, rising over the beat. I search the room. All I can see is the fog enveloping every inch of the space around me. Throbbing, beating into my very being. Then without warning the noise ceases and I'm drenched in silence. I pry open my eyes again, wishing I could cradle my head in my hands, but they lie paralyzed at my side, immovable.

Click. Click.

My eyes shoot forward and I see a flash of charcoal dart across my vision to the right and then it's gone. Lost beyond my sight. My breathing quickens. The paper walls I build in my mind begin to crumble.

Where is it?

I continue to search the room, begging for some sign of the thing that haunts me. My eyes meet only the deathly-quiet mist moving among the ceiling and walls. I squint, peering at the fog, trying to distract myself. Maybe if I just ignore it everything will be fine, I'll wake up and it'll all be over.

Please be over!

As the fog writhes and pulses above me, I witness the red prints again. Wide swathes of crimson smear along the wall, like a long-lost soul begging to be free.

Then I feel it, a warm mist on my neck just below my right ear. I shiver and freeze inside. It comes again. A soft pressure pats against my bare stomach. It's cold and stiff as it presses against my flesh. A piercing sting slithers up my chest and explodes in my head. I silently scream. But nothing comes out.

Then I hear it.

"Are you ready?" The voice is quiet and raspy with a hellish glee.

I scream inside, bellowing with all the might that's in me, but the noise never breaks the surface. *No.* It's as if my voice stops at the back of my throat, but I hear a crackle. I try again, nothing.

"Good." The voice tickles my neck, an utter impiousness about its tone. It sounds like it's enjoying this.

I endeavor to scream again but my effort is cut short by a searing pain in my side as something sharp and foreign tears deep into my ribs just below my chest. I gasp inside, wanting desperately to look down and see the claws that are undoubtedly buried in my side. As quickly as they had pierced into my body, they jerk back. My body sways under their exit and before I can catch my breath, the claws drill back into my flesh.

Above me the creature's horrid face, a sunken skull with crimson eyes, jerks around to face me, looming over my face, peering intently into my soul through empty eyes.

This time the creature doesn't rip its claws out again. Instead I feel them moving, wrenching my insides back and forth in its grip. Pain sears up my spine and explodes in my head and a burst of nausea breaches my stomach, threatening to reach my mouth. I beg to scream, to release the pain. I beg without answer. An eternity of pain courses through my body as the creature's claws dig and twist and carve inside me.

Then, as if it had wreaked enough damage, it stops. The claws stop moving, but I can still feel them clutching firmly to something under my chest. Every little movement, every subtle twitch, sends a new explosion of pain to my brain.

Wake up, Taren! Wake up!

Out of the corner of my vision I spy another figure stepping into view, shaded in the same dingy black sinew. My eyes widen.

There's more of them? No, no, no!

I cry inside, begging for it to stop, begging to wake up, for it all just to end. It doesn't seem to notice me yet, but that does nothing to squelch my fear. I squint under the pressure of the claws moving inside my body and at the strange gait of the new creature.

Is it limping?

A series of loud percussions deafen me. Before I have time to think, the pain in my side flashes to an intensity I had yet to experience as the claws rip out, tearing at my flesh. I groan inside, unable to scream, unable to clutch my burning side. I scream internally, cinching my eyes shut as the intense pain overwhelms my senses. I jerk my eyes back open and shoot them to the right. It's gone, the deathly figure is gone.

The fog around me dissipates, vanishing before my eyes. The walls of my room fade back to their dull whites. With agonizingly slow efficiency, I feel my arm move, then my leg. My breathing comes in spurts and my mouth trembles. A small reprieve reaches into my mind as my fear and agony escapes through those hectic tremors. Gaining control of my lips and vocal chords, I scream with everything that's in me! Despite the pain that still flows through my body, just hearing my voice gushing from my mouth is a relief.

What?

My side still hurts, it burns and the pain I felt in my dream still throbs in my side.

What the hell? Why does it hurt? How does it hurt?

Before I have time to process the reality of the pain tormenting my gut, I hear movement to my left. It's where the second thing, the second creature had stood just a heartbeat ago. I freeze, then force myself to look. But my eyes are not prepared for what they find. Where it had stood, where it had limped into the room, my eyes find Matt. Blood pours from his chest and a deep gash lines his shoulder, a pistol clutched in his hand, bloodied, and shaking. I peer up at him, confused and scared.

I can sense the fear in his eyes though I can barely see them looking right back at me. I can feel the unease and horror in them. He falters. I try to get up, but my body hasn't fully recovered from the paralysis. I tumble to my shoulder, terror overriding the pain my side.

"Matt!" I finally get the words out of my mouth, searching for an answer. "What? Matt."

"Tar…" he stutters as his body drops to the floor. His head bangs against the hardwood and his eyes flutter in and out.

I drop my eyes to where Matt's body lies crumpled on the floor, his arms haphazardly strewn above and below his body, his cheek pressed awkwardly against the hardwood as blood pools around his head and body. I can't find the words to say as his consciousness wavers.

"Taren." His voice is weak as he searches for me. Before I can speak, his body goes limp and his eyes, somehow, lose their glimmer.

"No, no, no, no!" I scream, gaining control over my body again and slinging my legs over the edge of the bed.

An intense burst of pain bores up my spine and crashes me back to the bed, flat again, prone, writhing in pain. I gasp, breathing in choking gasps. The burning had come from my side. I squint and raise myself, taking my time this time. For the first time, I peer down at my body.

"Oh my god!"

I fight the panic as I my eyes register the gaping hole in my side. There's so much blood. My side is ripped open, torn apart. Shreds of crimson-coated skin drape over my open flank. The pain is constant, coursing through my body. My blood drenches the mattress, creating a sea of red around me. I dare to touch the wound, but fear wrenches my hand back before I can do it.

Despite the pain, something catches my attention next to the bed. My eyes dart to a new object lying there in a familiar reddened circle. There's a body, a man, probably in his late thirties, collapsed on the floor, his head craned horribly against the wall. His arms hang limp over his chest and waist, his legs are sprawled out before him. His head hangs low, but I can still see his face. It's deathly cold. Mouth wide open, eyes glazed over, blood dripping from his lips. Two bullet holes pepper the body's chest, and a blood coated blade lies limply in his hand.

My demon?

My breathing stutters, threatening to get out of control again, but I force myself to rein it in. I avert my eyes from the gruesome sight, from the knife that had dug into my side, and find the blood flowing from my body. My eyes dart over the bed and my mind races.

I've got to stop the bleeding!

Grasping at the first thought my brain spat out, I curl the sheets below me in my fingers and wrap the thin, blood-soaked cloth around my waist. I wince with each movement as the fabric scrapes and presses against my open side. I shake my head, I'm beginning to feel lightheaded.

The blood temporarily contained, I slide off the bed and to my feet. I stand there staring at Matt's lifeless form for at least half a minute. The blood at my side has already soaked through the layers of sheets wrapped around me, but I just keep looking. How can it be? How?

I wipe my eyes, pushing back the tears, and clenching my fists against my body. With a deep gulp, I force my gaze away from Matt's body and step forward. I stop beside him, but I don't know what to say.

"Matt…" I start. A long second later I manage to get out two more words. "Thank you."

He'd given everything for me. Everything, and here I stand.

There's nothing you could have done, Taren. Nothing!

I push forward, immediately wrenching over in pain as the pieces of flesh at my side move and grate under the blanket. I grit my teeth, cutting off a scream. Propping myself against the door frame, I peer out into the dark hallway.

I reach for the light switch and flip on the lights. I immediately regret it. Down the hallway is more blood. My eyes trace the crimson trail from my room all the way down the hall and into the living room. I lean against the wall and force myself to move. Foot by foot I creep closer to the open living space. Every step brings down an avalanche of dread falling onto my core and a tidal wave of nauseating pain through my body.

A hand sliding against the wall, I press on, pushing myself farther down the hall. I groan at the pain grinding in my side. I refrain from checking the sheet that holds back my innards, not wanting to know how bad it looks.

I slouch against the wall; not sure I can stand to look around the bend. I close my eyes, seeking out the courage to move somewhere deep inside myself. I want to turn around, but only darkness is behind me. I can't turn back so I swallow and push myself forward. My eyes beg to close the moment I take in the open space, but instead I keep them open, wide, and horrified.

Asher and Rohan's bodies lie sprawled out in a bloodied mess on the sofa. My entire frame quivers and my feet shake underneath me. My food threatens to rise up my throat, but I hold it down. A long bloody line is carved through Rohan's skull just above his nose all the way up to the back of his head where the same knife that had pierced my side had apparently cleaved through his skull. A spider web of crimson drips down his nose and mouth. Asher lies back against the sofa, a look of pure horror permanently etched on his face. His left hand is half missing, the other piece, or pieces, strewn across the sofa and floor. A mass of blood soaks his chest.

I can't stand it anymore, I wretch, vomiting on the floor. My head feels light, like it's floating above this disgusting scene straight out of a movie. My stomach is uneasy, churning. I struggle to calm my breathing but nothing works. At the hem of the thin sheet covering my body, rivulets of blood run over the edge, splattering against the floor.

I have to call for help! I'm not dying like this!

Slapping a hand against the wall, I drag myself back along my bloody trail leading back to my room. I pause.

He's in there though.

My mind is murky but it races. I can't go back in there, I just can't do it. My hand begins to slip, but I get my grip again. But I need my phone. It's my only hope.

I urge myself forward. Blood smears against the wall from my palm as I pull myself down the hallway. My vision blurs, but then it comes back. I work to blink away the drowsiness that plagues me as my heart beats faster.

I falter, feet from the door. My body falls hard to the floor, slamming my wounded side against the hardwood. I scream in agony. Pain shoots through my side, overloading my senses.

No! Get up!

Gripping the doorframe, I haul myself back to my feet, letting the blanket fall like the flag of a defeated army. I let out a solid grunt as it rips away from my side and tumbles to the ground.

Blood gushes from my tattered side but I refuse to look. My head bobs as my body becomes light beneath me and my vision blurs again. I blink, but it doesn't help. The open doorway to my room is fuzzy and I swear it's swaying back and forth. I try again to steady myself and finally some clarity returns as I will myself forward.

My foot hits something and I go tumbling forward, face first to the floor. My head bangs against the stiff floor. I shake my head, clearing my vision, and reaching to rub my bruised cheek. Right before me are Matt's cold green eyes. I shiver and rip my gaze away as my head wobbles. Had I been standing I surely wouldn't have been for long.

Ignoring the pain and dizziness, I turn my body over, dragging my exposed wound over the floor. Pain sears up my side. I scream as strips of my torn flesh stick to the floor and are stretched, ripping new ribbons of skin from my waist. I strain to regulate my breathing, but it's no use. It comes in quick sudden gasps as I finally catch sight of my objective, my cell phone on the end table next to the bed.

I grip the floor with all that's left in me and drag my body painfully against the ground toward the table. Only a few feet to go. I heave again, but a sudden bout of dizziness stops me in my tracks. The world around me spins, my phone seems to be so much farther away than just seconds earlier.

I blink and squint, one more attempt to clear my head and ignore the pain. I can't, it's too much. As every nerve in my body throbs, I refuse to stop. Despite the pain, I gain control of my arms again and fight back the light-headedness. I pull myself closer. Almost there. Another inch. I reach out, lying on the ground. My finger grazes the thin device. Another inch. Finally, I grip it between my fingers and yank it to the floor. I almost lose my grip as my body quakes, but my fingers obey and hold tight.

Through the blotches of color and fuzzy shades of gray that shadow my eyes, I fumble with the phone, trying to swipe open the screen. Streaks of blood paint the device like a gruesome Picasso. My body quivers, then convulses, and I drop the phone. Pain sears through my core. I can't even muster the will to scream.

I reach out weakly one more time and slide the phone next to my face. I can feel the blood oozing from my mouth with each labored breath. I tap the phone frantically, but my fingers move in slow motion. With one last heavy finger, the screen comes to life, showing a simple dial pad. I keep my fingers moving.

9…1…

My hand drops before I can tap the last digit. It's like all the strength in my body has vanished. With each labored breath, my body convulses. I can't give up. I tap the screen again, ignoring the pain.

1… Send.

I fall fully onto my chest and let my arm drop limp to the ground as the call goes out. I listen to the ringing as my vision becomes useless and the world around me begins to cave into darkness. I fight to keep my eyes open, to search for the light of my phone on the floor, but it keeps getting darker.

"911, what is your emerg…" the voice is small and faint as it fades into nothing and my world wraps in around me.

ABOUT THE AUTHOR

Jordon Greene is the Award-Winning & Amazon Bestselling Horror Author of *To Watch You Bleed* and *They'll Call It Treason*. He is a full stack web developer for the nation's largest privately owned shoe retailer and a graduate of UNC Charlotte. Jordon spends his time building web applications, attempting to sing along to his favorite rock songs, reading and, of course, writing. He lives in Concord, NC just close enough and just far enough away from Charlotte.

Visit Jordon Online
www.JordonGreene.com

If you enjoyed this story,
please consider reviewing it and telling others about it.